Samuel French Acting Edition

The Winter Wife

by Claire Tomalin

I0591759

‖ SAMUEL FRENCH ‖

SAMUELFRENCH.COM   SAMUELFRENCH.CO.UK

FOR PRODUCTION ENQUIRIES

UNITED STATES AND CANADA
Info@SamuelFrench.com
1-866-598-8449

UNITED KINGDOM AND EUROPE
Plays@SamuelFrench.co.uk
020-7255-4302

Each title is subject to availability from Samuel French, depending upon
country of performance. Please be aware that THE WINTER WIFE may
not be licensed by Samuel French in your territory. Professional and
amateur producers should contact the nearest Samuel French office or
licensing partner to verify availability.

MUSIC USE NOTE

Licensees are solely responsible for obtaining formal written permission from copyright owners to use copyrighted music in the performance of this play and are strongly cautioned to do so. If no such permission is obtained by the licensee, then the licensee must use only original music that the licensee owns and controls. Licensees are solely responsible and liable for all music clearances and shall indemnify the copyright owners of the play(s) and their licensing agent, Samuel French, against any costs, expenses, losses and liabilities arising from the use of music by licensees. Please contact the appropriate music licensing authority in your territory for the rights to any incidental music.

IMPORTANT BILLING AND CREDIT REQUIREMENTS

If you have obtained performance rights to this title, please refer to your licensing agreement for important billing and credit requirements.

The first performance of *The Winter Wife* was given at the Nuffield Theatre, Southampton, on 12 February 1991. It transferred to the Lyric Theatre, Hammersmith on 5 March 1991. The cast was as follows:

IDA .... Gabrielle Lloyd
KATHERINE ....Rachel Joyce
MARIE ....Pamela Ruddock
DR. BOUCHAGE .... Michael Irving

Directed by Patrick Sandford. Designed by Tanya McCallin. Lighting by Stephen Watson, and stage management by Mandi Upward. In this production there were two non-speaking parts, Georgia Bance as a nurse and Mark Raggett as a porter.

CHARACTERS

KATHERINE MANSFIELD (Mrs. John Middleton Murry), aged 31

IDA CONSTANCE BAKER, aged 32

DR. BOUCHAGE, aged about 35

MARIE, aged about 50

(While the characters are based on real people and events, the play is in no sense a biography of Katherine Mansfield.)

SETTINGS

A compartment of a French *wagon-lit*, a doctor's surgery and the Villa Isola Bella, a simple holiday house in Menton on the French Riviera. The stage should show all three part of the villa, *salon*, terrace and a few steps leading up to the bedroom.

The time is 1920.

ACT I

Scene 1: The train

Scenes 2, 3: The villa

Scene 4: The surgery of Dr. Bouchage

Scenes 5, 6, 7: The villa

ACT II

Scene 1: The surgery

Scenes 2 – 6: The villa

Scene 7: A station platform

ACT I

Scene 1

We hear that we are inside a TRAIN—French Express, 1920. At first we can see nothing.

IDA. Did you call me, Katie?

(No answer. A small LIGHT goes on, illuminating an upper bunk bed, and we see the inside of the sleeping compartment. IDA is peering over the edge of the top bunk with an anxious face. SHE has her long hair sensibly tied back in a plait, and is wearing a practical flannel nightdress.)

IDA. Would you like me to rub your back, Katie dear?

(More silence. IDA hesitates, withdraws into her bunk, hesitates again, switches off her LIGHT. Now, from the lower bunk, KATHERINE (silk nightdress) very cautiously reaches out and half raises the blind so that SHE can see the countryside in the early morning LIGHT of September. The effort of raising the blind makes HER start coughing. As SHE coughs, we glimpse the LANDSCAPE of Provence rushing past. All the LIGHT is now in the lower part of the compartment.

9

IDA. (*From the darkness above.*) Are you all right, Katie?

(*No answer. KATHERINE struggles to control her cough.*)

IDA. Katie? Do you need some water?
KATHERINE. No.
IDA. Are you sure, dear?
KATHERINE. (*Coughing more, exasperated.*) *No!*

(*After a short pause, IDA's bare legs appear, dangling over the upper bunk. SHE climbs awkwardly and slowly down, feeling her way with her dangling legs. KATHERINE watches, fascinated. SHE is no longer coughing. IDA puts on her dressing gown and slips out of the compartment.*)

KATHERINE. She dropped down, slowly waving her big grey legs, as though something pulled her, dragged her—the tangle of rich blue weed on the red carpet luxuriously provided by the *chemins de fer de France* : (*KATHERINE's tone changes from dreamy to angry.*) What I feel is: she is never for one fraction of a second unconscious of me. If I sigh, I know that her head lifts. If I rustle my bedclothes, she pricks her ears and sits up. When we sit down together, I know that those grave large eyes solemnly fix on me. There is no escape. There is no chance of freedom. Even if I do absolutely nothing.

(*The TRAIN has slowed and stopped. IDA comes into the compartment again, peers under the window blind and announces.*)

IDA. (*Pronouncing French as English.*) A—vig ...
Avig ... Avig—non.
    KATHERINE. One of the loveliest names in the world
done to death. *Avignon. (Her French accent is excellent.)*

*(IDA turns and gazes at KATHERINE, who looks back at
    her totally expressionless, mask-like.)*

    IDA. Darling, I can see by your eyes that you have *not*
had a good night.

*(KATHERINE stares Ida out and, when IDA turns away,
    says, so suddenly that IDA jumps.)*

    KATHERINE. *Jones!* I'm all right. Just think about
getting us some breakfast.

ACT I

Scene 2

*The villa Isola Bella in Menton. We can see the hall-salon
    downstairs, MARIE (a neat, brisk but comfortable
    woman in an apron) and IDA carrying bags through and
    up the short flight of stairs into the bedroom.
    Meanwhile KATHERINE is standing in the doorway to
    the terrace, motionless and gazing out into the
    SUNSHINE. MARIE goes downstairs and disappears,
    leaving IDA to hover. Very slowly, KATHERINE turns*

and makes her way up the stairs. SHE is dressed with perfect taste, every detail right, from hat to shoes. Entering her room, SHE takes no notice of Ida, just stands surveying her new territory.

IDA. I'll do your unpacking as soon as you like, Katie dear. Would you like to lie down for a bit? Or will you wait until after tea? Oh, good, there are some mosquito nets.

KATHERINE. I'll have tea first. There's no hurry about unpacking. You can do it later, after tea.

IDA. You must be awfully tired. Tired and hot. Strange that it's autumn in England, and like a furnace here in Mentone. (*SHE gives the English pronunciation.*)

KATHERINE. I *love* this heat. *Menton*, Ida.

(MARIE comes in with another bag, and repeats approvingly.)

MARIE. *Menton, mais oui, Mesdames. Quelle belle ville. Quelle chaleur.* (*Exit.*)

KATHERINE. The sun gets right into my bones and makes me feel better. All that English damp was killing me. I can't think why I ever tried to live in England. Just look at the view! (*SHE pushes open the long window, revealing brilliant blue, and stands with her back to Ida. SHE goes on speaking.*) Off you go, Ida, thank you. I'll come when tea is ready.

IDA. Are you sure you're all right, Katie? You wouldn't like me to bring you some warm water? Or some cool water?

KATHERINE. (*Mimicking her.*) Or some ice, Katie dear? Or how about a nice little bowl of cyanide? Just go away, Ida, that's all.

(*IDA goes. When she has gone, KATHERINE turns round slowly, and extracts a photograph of her husband from a small bag, puts it on the table beside her bed, pauses to look at it. SHE speaks to him, quite conversationally, pausing between sentences as though he were actually present and might answer.*)

KATHERINE. If only you were not tied by your work. If only, if only … The villa seems quite perfect. A narrow leafy way up from the station, a view of the sea. Terrific heat. That's bliss. I shall be able to live on the terrace all day, and here by my window at night. The only dark spot on my happiness is that you are not here. I want to share all this with you. Not with anyone else, *with you alone.* Remember that.

(*While she is speaking, we see MARIE putting out tea things downstairs, and IDA rearranging them.*)

IDA. Tea, Katie, when you're ready!
KATHERINE. (*Puts her finger to the lips of the photograph. Then SHE takes out some of her books.*) Here is my Keats. Here is my Coleridge. And my Shakespeare. My notebooks. Jane Austen. And what's this one? Oh, *Bleak House.* (*SHE looks for a passage, turning the pages, smiling.*)

(IDA is coming up again, uncertainly, this time bearing a small pot of flowers from the tea table, which SHE puts on the chest of drawers.)

IDA. Would you like your tea here? Only I'm afraid there's no cake.

KATHERINE. Cake? No. Thank you, Ida. I'll come down in a few minutes. You go and pour if you like.

IDA. Well. I'll go down and wait for you. We can always make another pot. If you're quite sure you don't need me here. *(And goes again.)*

(When she has gone, KATHERINE arranges her books and takes the flowers from where Ida put them, moving them to sit next to the photograph of Murry. Then SHE goes to the door and starts down the short flight of stairs towards her tea.)

ACT I

Scene 3

Late morning, hot SUNSHINE on the terrace outside the villa. A palm tree beyond the balustrade, mimosa not yet in bloom, roses etc. KATHERINE is standing, leaning on her stick, beside the chaise longue, which IDA is trying to arrange in a position that will please her.

KATHERINE. I shall need a table next to the *chaise longue*, for my books and papers. I shall need a rug of some kind, and cushions. And I think I shall have to have some sort of umbrella or parasol, if I'm not to fry and frizzle like one of the martyrs: don't you think, Jones? Though that's perhaps the way you really think of me, old Jonesie, eh?

IDA. You know I don't, darling.

KATHERINE. Just a tiny bit of frizzling round the edges for Kass, though, you don't mind that too much, do you? Just so that you can relish sprinkling the holy water on me.

IDA. Katie, you know perfectly well that my one wish is to help you get better.

KATHERINE. I know about the *helping* part. I'm not quite so convinced about the getting better.

IDA. You don't mean to say these things, I know, but—

KATHERINE. I *do* mean to say them, and I do, *mean* them, don't you forget it. I know all about your yearning and doting and wanting to have me at your mercy. I've seen that in you from the very first. From the first day when you appeared on the stairs at school, all yearning and miserable and ready to take over my life, and jealous of anyone else who came near me—

(*At this point MARIE starts to emerge from the house, with something on a tray—perhaps a small bunch of grapes in a bowl of water—intended for Katherine. Sensing that this is a bad moment, SHE stops and retreats into the doorway, but cannot resist watching the rest of the scene.*)

IDA. Never jealous! Never! It's not in my nature to be jealous. It's simply that we were friends, from the beginning, and that friendship means something special and sacred to me. Of course I want you to get better more than anything in the world.

KATHERINE. And when I *am* better, make no mistake, I shan't have you creeping and crawling round me with trays and hot water bottles, and cushions and deck chairs, and medicine glasses, and shawls to put over my shoulders. (*SHE is almost shouting by the end of this speech, her face distorted with anger.*) Creepy crawly! Creeping and crawling, and stuffing yourself with food to set me a fine example! Creeping and crawling and stuffing yourself! Pushing yourself in where you're not wanted!

IDA. (*Softly.*) Katie, Katie ...

KATHERINE. I *loathe* you, Ida, make no mistake about it. I abominate everything about you. With your chocolate in your pocket, and your great slabs of cake for tea. You should never have tried to come with me to France It makes me ill just to have you here.

IDA. (*With dignity.*) Katie, Katie, you'll *make* yourself ill like that. And remember we are going to the doctor this afternoon.

(*KATHERINE screams at her. SHE screams until IDA exits to the house, passing the surprised MARIE with what dignity SHE can.*)

IDA. Madame is not well today.

(*MARIE merely gestures.*

KATHERINE, when she has finished screaming, gives
    herself a shake and sits down. SHE is surprised at
    herself.)

ACT I

Scene 4

DR. BOUCHAGE is washing his hands in his surgery, a
    very plain cream-painted room with desk, screen,
    examination couch, wash basin, scales for weighing
    patients, window high up with opaque glass. It is all
    functional, not luxurious. HE is about thirty-five, thin
    and intelligent-looking, with a bright, eager expression.
    HIS English is perfect (in case anyone asks, he worked
    with English troops during the ware when he was a
    medical officer). The door of his surgery is opened
    discreetly by his NURSE, and KATHERINE is shown
    in. SHE is smartly dressed and made up, and is in a
    good mood again. BOUCHAGE advances and takes her
    hand, looking at her intently. SHE returns the gaze.

BOUCHAGE. Mrs. Murry: please come and sit down,
and tell me how I can be of service to you.
KATHERINE. Dr. Bouchage. I have a premonition that
you are the doctor who is going to cure me miraculously
and completely of all my ailments.
BOUCHAGE. That will of course be my endeavor. But
first we must become acquainted.

KATHERINE. You will ask me the usual questions, and I shall give you the usual answers. Or perhaps I'll give you unusual answers for a change. You will ask what is the matter with me. I'll tell you I am suffering from the second decade of the twentieth century. It gives me spots in my lungs.

BOUCHAGE. Ah, Mrs. Murry, you are a quick diagnostician. I must go more slowly. Tell me: you are here in Menton for your health?

(KATHERINE nods.)

BOUCHAGE. You are here with your husband?

KATHERINE. No, I am here without my husband. I am here with my ... housekeeper. My husband would be here if he could, *of course*, but unfortunately he has to stay in London. He is the editor of a weekly magazine. It is impossible for him to get away.

BOUCHAGE. *(Who is making the occasional note as they talk.)* A weekly magazine! That's very interesting. A political magazine?

KATHERINE. No, a literary magazine. He is a critic, and a poet; and I am a writer, so I can work anywhere.

BOUCHAGE. You yourself are a writer? You write novels, poetry?

KATHERINE. I write stories mostly.

BOUCHAGE. So you have a special temperament. The temperament of an artist. And now I must go back a little, Mrs. Murry. You are a Londoner—you were born in London?

KATHERINE. No, I am not a Londoner. I am a ... colonial. I was born at the furthest point of the world at which you can still be British: in New Zealand.

BOUCHAGE. Aha—so you are also a traveller. And the year of your birth, please, Mrs. Murry?

KATHERINE. I was born in 1888. A stormy evening in October. Worse, I was a third daughter.

BOUCHAGE. Is there any history of ill health in your family?

KATHERINE. My father is a stout and healthy man. My mother died two years ago. She had a weak heart.

BOUCHAGE. Brothers and sisters?

KATHERINE. Three sisters, all healthy. One brother, killed in the war.

BOUCHAGE. I am sorry.

KATHERINE. It is a common affliction. Perhaps you served in the war too?

BOUCHAGE. Indeed. It allowed me at least to practise my English. And your own health as a child? Were you always so slender as you are now?

KATHERINE. (*Laughing.*) Believe it or not, I was a fat child. My mother hated me for being so fat. "You haven't lost any weight, have you, Kass?... *Still* as fat as ever, Kass?" was all she ever said to me. I was the Cinderella. She'd be pleased now, anyway.

BOUCHAGE. And you left New Zealand ...?

KATHERINE. My father brought us to school in England when I was fourteen—for three years—in London—and then I *hated* going back to Wellington. And finally I managed to return to London, alone. And I've lived in Europe ever since.

BOUCHAGE. And you were married in—

KATHERINE. I was married in 1912.

BOUCHAGE. Your husband is quite healthy?

KATHERINE. Apart from the fact that he works too hard and doesn't look after himself ...

BOUCHAGE. Children?

KATHERINE. No children. I *wanted* children. I *still* want children.

BOUCHAGE. Any miscarriages?

KATHERINE. No.

BOUCHAGE. You have never been pregnant?

KATHERINE. Well. In fact, yes. I did lose a baby once.

BOUCHAGE. Which year was this?

KATHERINE. *I* was twenty.

BOUCHAGE. (*Notes silently.*) And the trouble with your lungs began after this?

KATHERINE. Long after. Not until 1917—during the war, in winter. I had one or two bouts of pleurisy, and fever, and the doctor in London strapped up my chest so that I could hardly move!

BOUCHAGE. And since 1917?

KATHERINE. Since 1917, I have been trying to get better.

BOUCHAGE. You have seen many different doctors? You have been in a sanatorium?

KATHERINE. Many doctors, yes. Sanatorium, no. It would be quite simply kill me to go into a sanatorium, Dr. Bouchage. You see, I have to be free to work. And I must be with my husband—at least some of the time.

BOUCHAGE. So. You have lost weight, over these years. Are you much troubled with coughing?

KATHERINE. Yes. Sometimes I cough blood. Not much. I have a lot of pain in my back. In my arms and legs. In my feet, even. I have headaches, and fever. It is difficult to sleep at night. But I am determined to get better. What do you think, Dr. Bouchage?

BOUCHAGE. (*Smiles at her across his desk.*) The will of the patient is most important. Also the climate, the way of life; rest, good food, a regular routine. Perhaps I might now take your weight, and examine your chest, Mrs. Murry? There is a screen here, if you'd would remove your blouse; you will find a special garment to change into, on the table there.

(*KATHERINE goes behind the screen, emerging with a simple cotton halter top that covers her breasts. BOUCHAGE leads her to his scales and proceeds to weigh her carefully and notes her weight, which is about 40 kilos. Then HE begins to auscult, tapping her back and listening. HE asks HER to cough. BOTH preserve expressionless faces during this procedure, but as HE finishes HE motions to her that she should dress again.*)

KATHERINE. (*From behind screen.*) I believe you are the youngest doctor who has ever examined me. In England all my doctors have grey beards and silk hats.

BOUCHAGE. (*Washing his hands.*) Silk hats! Indeed. I regret I cannot oblige you with a silk hat. The grey beard I expect quite soon. (*HE makes more notes while KATHERINE dresses again.*)

KATHERINE. (*Still behind the screen.*) Oh, Ida must have my comb. Could we call her, Dr. Bouchage, she is in your waiting room?

BOUCHAGE. By all means. (*As HE goes towards the door, HE turns back to Katherine to ask.*) Ida ...?

KATHERINE. Miss Baker. My housekeeper. She is my winter companion.

BOUCHAGE. Ah! Miss Baker is your *companion*. She reads aloud to you, and takes down your letters.

KATHERINE. It's only in novels that companions take down letters, Dr. Bouchage. I write my own letters. Ida's companionship is more of—more of an irritant in my daily life.

(*Calling her for herself, as BOUCHAGE goes towards the door and politely murmurs round it.*)

KATHERINE. *Ida*!

(*IDA enters, going straight past Bouchage and ignoring his politely proffered hand, to find Katherine. KATHERINE makes the introduction from the screen, IDA politely returning to BOUCHAGE to shake hands, and returning to Katherine at once.*)

KATHERINE. Ida—this is Dr. Bouchage—Dr. Bouchage, Miss Baker. Dr. Bouchage is going to cure me with sunshine and olive oil. (*In a lower voice.*) You have my comb, Jones.

(IDA passes her bag to Katherine for her to extract a comb, which SHE does, and uses deftly and quickly to arrange her hair.)

IDA. If there are any questions of diet, Dr. Bouchage, you have only to explain them to me and I shall make sure they are carried out exactly as you say.

BOUCHAGE. Miss Baker, I am sure you realize that Mrs. Murry must eat well—milk, and butter, and eggs, and fruit, and good meat. And she must rest, no worries, no exertion, just rest and food and sunshine whenever possible.

IDA. The trouble is, of course, Doctor, she will not rest. She is always working.

BOUCHAGE. Working? What is this work, Mrs. Murry?

KATHERINE. *(Handing IDA back her bag with a warning look, then turning to Bouchage.)* I did explain to you, Dr. Bouchage, that I am a writer.

IDA. It's not just your writing, though, Katie dear, is it, it's all those reviews. She gets these huge parcels of books, Dr. Bouchage, and she has to read them all, sometimes four or five at a time, and write about them.

KATHERINE. *(Furious.)* Be quiet, Jones.

(BOUCHAGE registers this.)

KATHERINE. *(Turns to him.)* This is work for my husband, for his magazine.

IDA. No magazine can be as important as your health, Kass.

KATHERINE. It is simply none of your business, Jones. Dr. Bouchage: if I do not work, I might as well be dead, it's as simple as that.

BOUCHAGE. (*Looking from one to the other.*) Perhaps you could work a little less hard, all the same, Mrs. Murry. I'm sure your husband will understand that there is good reason. Supposing you limited yourself to two hours of work, and then rested? And Miss Baker will bring you a drink of milk, something to eat? You have a good cook at Isola Bella?

KATHERINE. We have a charming cook: Marie.

IDA. She is very expensive, of course, but—

BOUCHAGE. So—you will eat well, you will rest as much as possible, you will take sunbaths, and I shall see you again next week. If you have any need of me meanwhile, you have only to send a messenger and I shall come to you at Isola Bella.

(*KATHERINE and IDA go out together, murmuring polite goodbyes, though KATHERINE is evidently angry with Ida, and IDA is nervously defiant. BOUCHAGE, seeing them out, is clearly intrigued by the English ladies.*)

ACT I

Scene 5

IDA and MARIE arranging the terrace to Katherine's requirements, struggling to put up the new parasol together. THEY are not natural allies. MARIE has no

English, IDA virtually no French. Then IDA spreads a fur rug on the chaise longue, and MARIE brings cushions and a table. IDA arranges flowers on the table. MARIE brings out another canvas chair. IDA now fishes in her pocket for a small sheaf of household bills.

IDA. By the way, Marie, this is definitely more than we should be spending on butter. *Trop de beurre. Trop cher.* And what do we need wine for? *Pourquoi vin?*

MARIE. *Mais—Meess—pour faire la sauce! Vous ne voulez pas quand-même que je serve le poisson de Madame sans sauce! Madame qui a surtout besoin d'être bien nourrie. Et puis les bonnes sauces ne se font pas sans beurre; sans crème; sans un verre de vin blanc.*

IDA. It is perfectly possible to eat well without this sort of expense. Sauces can be made with cornflour. *Farine.* We shall have to economize.

MARIE. *Madame est pourtant bien contente de ma cuisine.*

IDA. *Madame* would not be so *contente* if she saw these bills.

MARIE. (*Gallic shrug, scornful.*) *Ah, Meess ... Madame est si mince, si frêle. On voit bien qu'elle a besoin de plats délicats.*

(The voice of KATHERINE is heard from upstairs.)

KATHERINE. Has the post come?

IDA. Not yet, dear. I'll bring it up as soon as it comes.

KATHERINE. I'm coming down in any case.

IDA. (*To Marie.*) Thank you, Marie. We shall have to go through these accounts later.

KATHERINE. (*As SHE passes Marie in the salon,
SHE pats her arm and says.*) *Vous pouvez faire ma
chambre, Marie.*

(*And MARIE goes up with a duster, etc. KATHERINE
goes out on to the terrace, sits down and starts to read.
IDA goes back into the house, and up to Katherine's
bedroom, to find MARIE dusting the table on which the
photograph of Murry stands.*)

MARIE. *C'est le mari de madame? Beau jeune homme!*
IDA. Thank you, Marie, I always do Madame's room.
(*And SHE firmly steers the surprised MARIE out. SHE
spends some time straightening things and making the bed,
which now has billowing, old-fashioned, white mosquito
nets. As SHE smoothes it, SHE murmurs.*) There, my
lovely. There. (*SHE hangs up and folds various garments.
It is evident that SHE regards the room as some sort of
shrine. When she had finished worshipping, SHE goes
downstairs and out onto the terrace again, standing at some
distance, watching KATHERINE, who is now writing.
IDA thinks herself unobserved.*)
KATHERINE. (*Suddenly.*) I've decided I'm going to
keep a journal of our time here at the villa. I'm telling Jack
to expect it to be ready for the publishers by Christmas.
It's going to be dead true, and light-hearted. Perhaps I'll put
you into it, Jones, so you'd better prepare yourself. You
may be about to become famous, and your little struggles
with Marie will pass into literature.

(*KATHERINE says all this without looking at Ida, but her
tone is friendly as well as mocking, and IDA looks*

*relieved as well as amused. Now MARIE appears, with
a cup of bouillon for Katherine.)*

MARIE. *(Not looking at Ida.) Voilà pour madame.*
KATHERINE. *(Perfect French, perfect accent, smiling.)
Merci, ma bonne Marie! Quel plaisir!*

*(The BELL rings. MARIE hurries to answer it, returning
with three letters which SHE attempts to give
Katherine, but IDA intercepts her and takes them.)*

MARIE. *Le facteur, madame.*
KATHERINE. *(Looks at the three envelopes. Two fail
to interest her, but the third SHE wants very much. But
SHE will wait until she is alone to read it. SHE turns to
Marie.) Alors, ça s'est bien passé au marché ce matin?*
MARIE. *Ah, vous savez, madame, depuis la guerre tout
est affreusement cher. Deux francs cinquante pour un
choufleur pas plus gros qu'une tomate. (SHE shows its
size with her hands.)*

(KATHERINE laughs, IDA cannot understand.)

IDA. There are some problems in the kitchen, Kass.
Not for you to worry about, but problems—*(SHE gestures
to signify there is more than she likes to say.)*
KATHERINE. *(Laughing, and refusing Ida's signals.)*
Well, these are dangerous times we are living in. *(To
Marie.) J'explique à mademoiselle que les temps sont
dangereux. Mais on doit continuer à manger des
chouxfleurs, à tout prix, n'est-ce pas? (To Ida.)* We can't

live without cauliflowers, can we, even in these dangerous times?

(IDA is baffled by the teasing.)

MARIE. *Madame a parfaitement raison. (And MARIE goes into the house, satisfied.)*

(KATHERINE starts to read her letters.)

ACT I

Scene 6

The terrace again. KATHERINE is on the chaise longue, referring to one of her books, crossing out a phrase, pulling faces at herself.

KATHERINE. *(Muttering as SHE writes.)* "We have read this kind of thing so often that it produces no impression at all ..."

IDA. *(Comes out of the French windows, bearing parcels from her shopping expedition.)* Is that the journal?

KATHERINE. *(Imitating her.)* Is that the journal? No, it's not the journal, it's a frightful review of a lot of frightfully trashy books by a lot of frightfully well-considered writers. That'll show them.

IDA. I wonder why Jack doesn't send you the interesting books?

KATHERINE. Never mind that. He sends me interesting letters anyway.

IDA. I'm glad, darling. Now look what I've brought for us. I thought we might try some of this specially good coffee. Marie told me where to get it. Just smell the packet! And these are your cigarettes.

(KATHERINE fishes for money, IDA waves it away.)

IDA. And I thought you might like this particularly beautiful peach. It was almost signalling to me, irresistible ... and in the market they were selling these little bowls, I thought you'd enjoy your peach even more out of one. *(SHE arranges a large and perfect peach in a brightly colored bowl, with a leaf, etc.)*

KATHERINE. Jones: I'm glad you noticed the peach signalling. Thank you, *ma chère*. I'm so hungry, I'll have it before lunch, I think. And lovely coffee! How extravagant you are. How delicious this all is.

(Pause, while IDA prepares to take her purchases into the house.)

KATHERINE. If you're feeling really rich today, Jones, could you stretch to making me a loan?

IDA. Of course, darling, what do you need? Let's see, I've got five francs here.

KATHERINE. It's really pounds I need, not francs.

IDA. Five *pounds*? That's quite a lot ...

KATHERINE. Actually, Jones dear, I need forty pounds.

IDA. Forty pounds ... *Forty* pounds? But Kass darling, without wanting to be awkward, that's an enormous amount of money suddenly. I mean, to find just like that.

KATHERINE. I was just wondering if you had any to spare. I never seem to have a penny, once I've paid the doctors, and the household bills; and you know how mean Jack is to me ... And now he has this man on his heels ...

IDA. You know I'm always ready to help you in any way I can; but I don't know that I can help *Jack* ...

KATHERINE. Never mind, never mind. I'll just have to find it some other way. I should be getting the advance on my book soon and, as it happens, the advance is exactly forty pounds ... I wonder if that is entirely a coincidence?

IDA. If what is a coincidence?

KATHERINE. The fact that he is asking for the exact amount of my advance. Could he have heard about it?

IDA. Could who have heard? Katie: I don't understand what you are talking about.

KATHERINE. Of course you don't, Jones dear, because you are not interested in my problems.

IDA. I don't know how you can say that.

KATHERINE. You don't know how I can say that ... You don't know very much, you don't know *anything* because you are totally lacking in understanding of friendship, or human need, of everything that makes two people understand one another.

(IDA walks away and stands with her back to Katherine, looking over the balustrade of the terrace.)

KATHERINE. If you want to know, I need this money really badly *now*. So that is why I thought of turning to my best friend.

IDA. (*Turning round, at once contrite.*) I am sorry if I seem to fail you.

KATHERINE. Never mind. Let me explain it to you so that you can understand. Something bad has happened. Do you remember Floryan—Floryan with the impossible Polish name, Floryan Sobieniowski? (*Pronounced, roughly, Sobyenyofski.*)

IDA. Floryan ... You mean your Polish admirer? The awful one who was always trying to borrow money? Oh—I don't mean ...

KATHERINE. Yes, well, he's not trying to borrow money now. He's trying to blackmail me.

IDA. How could he possible blackmail you, Katie? There's nothing you could have done that anyone could blackmail you about!

KATHERINE. No, well, of course not. But all the same, *he* thinks there is.

IDA. You must just ignore him, Kass. Take absolutely no notice. There's nothing he can do. You're going to be famous now, with your book coming out, you don't have to bother with people like that. Tell Jack to send him packing.

KATHERINE Yes. Only that's just it. You know what Jack is like. I can't bear the thought of him being bothered. And with my book coming out, I can't have Floryan talking to the newspapers, digging up old stories, showing old letters. Jones, I simply have to get those letters back and *burn them*.

IDA. (*Soothing*.) Of course, Katie, of course. I'll get them back if they matter so much. Only, are you really sure they do matter?

KATHERINE. They're letters I wrote to him when I was very young ... Silly letters, when he was in love with me, or fancied he was in love with me, you know, in Bavaria, before the war.

IDA. But Katie, if they're just old letters from so long ago, what possible harm can they do to anyone?

KATHERINE. (*Slowly*.) You don't understand. That was a very unhappy time for me. I don't want anything at all around to remind me of that time.

IDA. All the same, Kass dear.

KATHERINE. (*Furious again*.) How can you of all people fail to understand? *You* burned all my letters when I asked you to. I can't bear having people carrying round bits of my past. I don't belong to other people! I don't think you've ever understood what it meant to me, that time in Bavaria, losing the baby, being all alone, terrified of what was going to happen, not knowing whether I dared to come back to London even. I just don't want anything from that time to survive. We *must* find £40.

IDA So Floryan is asking £40 for your old letters ... but he must be mad, Katie! Surely Jack wouldn't let him do such a thing.

KATHERINE. Oh Jack ... he won't do anything, he just writes helplessly to me asking what I think. Of course *he* won't pay the money. But *I'd* pay the money. I'd give every penny I've got to get those letters back. Everything, every single thing about Floryan Sobieniowski fills me with disgust and horror. For one thing, Jones, he got me into a frightful trap. He gave me a German story; I did a version of it which got published later, and now it turns out it was really a Chekhov story. Quite a famous one. It could look as though I stole it from Chekhov. Floryan knows all about that. It could do me a lot of harm now if anyone chose to make something of it. Imagine the sniggers in Bloomsbury. And then Floryan made me ill too ...

IDA. (*Taking all this in slowly.*) Is it Jack you are worried about?

KATHERINE. Oh bother Jack. I don't suppose Jack is capable of understanding anything about this. No, I've got to deal with it. And you'll have to help me, Ida. You've always been the one to help me. I rely on you.

IDA. Well, of course we'll find the money. The important thing is for you to have peace, and if Jack can't cope with this, never fear, Jones can. I'll go and have a look at my bank balance ... And Katie, I'll bring out the thermometer. You look as though you might be feverish to me.

KATHERINE. (*Speaking slowly and dreamily.*) You know, Ida, being in love in Bavaria was like a game. Floryan was fearfully good-looking; and he was funny, with his bad German ... and bruised, and innocent at the same time. He said my red sweater was like a flower garden for him ... I thought there was going to be so much life then ... that it would all be experience I could use. I thought I could live all sorts of different lives, and be unscathed ...

IDA. People have *always* taken advantage of you.

KATHERINE. (*Taking no notice.*) Ida, when you travelled to Rhodesia, did you ever have troubles with men?

IDA. No, Katie. No, I didn't. Of course there were some nice young officers who played deck games with us ... but they weren't quite ... or I wasn't ... I don't think I *thought* about things like that.

KATHERINE. All the same: to think that Floryan is capable of behaving like this, after everything that happened then ... Well, I suppose it's all experience. (*SHE talks very slowly, more to herself than to Ida now.*) Only it's not *all* experience, is it, when you come to think about it? You grab at life, you want to try everything, but some of it is just waste ... waste, and destruction too. (*SHE shivers, and draws her rug round herself.*)

IDA. (*Sits at the end of the chaise longue, takes hold of one of Katherine's feet, and rubs it in an attempt to comfort her.*) Katherine: I will find the forty pounds somehow, and give it to you. But Jack must do the rest. He must go with Floryan to a solicitor, receive the letters, and get his sworn statement that he will never trouble you again. And as soon as Jack has those letters, he must post them off to you at once, so that you can destroy them.

KATHERINE. A bonfire. You're right, Ida, that is the only way. As the nights begin to get cooler, we'll warm ourselves with a bonfire.

ACT I

Scene 7

Evening in the salon/hall. IDA and KATHERINE are sitting together. IDA has an English newspaper and a

*book beside her, each of which SHE picks up and looks
at intermittently. KATHERINE is reading one of her
review books with ferocious concentration, making
occasional notes. Enter MARIE in her coat, about to
leave for the night.*

MARIE. *(Warmly.) Bonsoir. madame!* (And now
coolly, and with a touch of contempt.) *Bonsoir, Meess
Jones.* (To Katherine, with a big smile.) *Vous n'avez
besoin de rien, madame? Vous avez bien dîné, n'est-ce pas?*
KATHERINE. *Mais très bien, ma bonne Marie; nous
avons tout ce qu'il nous faut, Mademoiselle Ida et moi.
Allez. bonsoir, merci, à demain.*
IDA. Good night, Marie.

*(KATHERINE has turned straight back to her work. Pause,
while IDA scans her paper.)*

IDA. I see that the League of Nations is going to have
its headquarters in Geneva. There is going to be an
enormous palace there. Beside the lake. It will be very
pleasant for the diplomats, won't it? Sometimes I think
that must be the nicest possible career for a man. More
rewarding than being a doctor. Even an Army doctor like
Papa. There is more variety to the travel.

(KATHERINE goes on working.)

IDA. Perhaps we'll go and visit the site when we are in
Switzerland again—do you remember the dear old *pension*
Bieler? Those dreadful *compotes de fruits* Madame Bieler

used to serve at every meal! (*Pause.*) It says here Woodrow Wilson is likely to be awarded the Nobel Peace Prize.

(*KATHERINE makes assenting noise without raising her head from her work. IDA turns the pages of her paper. KATHERINE still working. Pause, then IDA continues.*)

IDA. I'm surprised Jack hasn't sent you those letters yet. How long has it been? Three weeks I think?

KATHERINE. (*Tight voice.*) Three and a half. Jack's always busy. He's got his tennis parties. His dinners. (*Brrrr ... Silence for a while.*)

IDA. (*Gets up and goes out on to the terrace, then comes back and picks up her book. Brightly.*) I haven't read your review of the Galsworthy, Katie, but I must say I am enjoying it *very much.* It's really lifelike. The Forsytes remind me of a family we used to know when Mother was alive. And there's something very clever about the way he fits in all the different cousins and uncles and aunts. Without getting them muddled up. Such a lot of them. (*Pause.*) Perhaps you should try making up a really long story, using all the same characters, a big family, people growing up and having children and getting married ... and divorced, of course ...

KATHERINE I'll bear your suggestion in mind if I should run out of inspiration.

IDA Oh, Katie, you know I didn't mean to imply that you would ever *need* any suggestions. I just thought Galsworthy had hit on rather a neat and perhaps quite a simple way of writing a story. It's so easy to follow. I mean, he makes it all very clear. He puts everything in.

You can't help liking Old Jolyon; and young Jolyon; and Uncle James. And Aunt Emily. Anyway, of course, you've already read it all.

KATHERINE. (*Acidly.*) And reviewed it. (*Starts to gather up her papers and books and rises laboriously to her feet. SHE makes towards the door and the stairs.*)

IDA. Are you going up so early? Kass, dear, you're not feeling unwell are you? Should I bring you a cold drink?

KATHERINE. (*Turning back from foot of stairs, and mimicking her.*) Or a hot drink? (*Then in a terrible voice.*) Ida: I have to work, in order to earn money. If I don't get my reviews done on time, I don't get any money. If I don't get the money, we shall starve, we shall not be able to afford the dangerously extravagant Marie and I shall not be able to pay Dr. Bouchage's bills or get any more medicine. I need medicine rather badly, and I need to be able to pay Dr. Bouchage, even if we both decide to stop eating, which is not something I notice you are inclined to do, however much you complain about the cook. If you talk to me while I am working, I can't get anything done. Since we are trapped in this house together, and since there seems no way of escaping your twittering except by shutting myself up in my room, that is what I propose to do. I am going upstairs.

IDA. (*Deeply mortified.*) I'm truly sorry, Kass, it was very inconsiderate of me. I'll be as quiet as a mouse.

KATHERINE No, no, why don't you try reading Galsworthy aloud another time? I might pick up a few tips from him. I might learn to "put everything in" too.

IDA. Oh, *Katie*! I didn't mean that at all!

KATHERINE. No? Anyway, I think I'll postpone that lesson until tomorrow. For the present I'll leave you to your solitary enjoyment of the master.

IDA. Katie, Katie, I know I'm a clumsy person, but—

KATHERINE. Never mind being clumsy. I do just sometimes wonder what ever possessed me to think we could have been friends or had anything at all in common in the first place. But never mind, never mind. On reflection, I might try advertising for a companion in *The Lady* next week. I doubt if they could come up with anything less congenial. (*And SHE goes painfully up the stairs, pausing on each step.*)

(*IDA watches her in agony. Twice SHE starts to go to help her but is daunted by a look of fury from KATHERINE. KATHERINE shuts her door. IDA begins to weep.*)

KATHERINE. (*Opens her door again.*) Jonesie, I'm sorry I lost my temper. I don't know quite what possessed me. Only I *do* have to work, you know, it's no good thinking I can sit and talk to you about the League of Nations, or Galsworthy. I just have to keep grinding. However worried I am. Whatever the failure of my husband to carry out my instructions. But it occurs to me that you might like to come and brush my hair for me later. It might help me to get to sleep. Drive away the demons.

IDA. Oh Katie … Of course I'd love to. I know I'm not clever, I'm a fool, but I didn't mean to …

KATHERINE. (*Quickly.*) Never mind, never mind. Just come and brush my hair for me. All right?

(And IDA goes off to fetch a small tray with milk and biscuits to take up to Katherine's room. Much fussing in and out, much fetching of towels from her unseen adjacent room, cologne, an array of brushes and combs, with KATHERINE also going in and out [of bathroom] and returning in dressing gown. While this is going on, KATHERINE hums snatches of Carmen. *Then.)*

KATHERINE. Did you read about the poison trial in the paper?

IDA. (*Concentrating on her arrangement of brushes.*) You mean the woman who's accused of poisoning her husband?

KATHERINE. Yes, that one.

IDA. She must be innocent. I can't believe a wife would do such a thing. Can you imagine a woman giving poison to her own husband? In this day and age?

KATHERINE. (*Brightly, from the bathroom.*) I'd say it's the exception to find couples who don't poison each other. (*Coming in again.*) The woman in the dock may be innocent enough, but the people in court are nearly all of them poisoners.

IDA. (*Dubiously.*) I've never met a poisoner.

KATHERINE. (*Enjoying this.*) The only reason why so many couples survive, is because one is *frightened* of giving the other the fatal dose. They just give tiny pinches and particles that settle in the toes, and work slowly up. Tiny parcels of hate.

IDA. I see what you mean ... at least I suppose ...

KATHERINE. (*Triumphantly.*) Both my husbands poisoned me! You are a witness, Ida!

IDA. (*Slightly nervous of all of this.*) Well, never mind. Here you are quite safe.

KATHERINE. It's not just husbands, you know. In every couple, there is one who devours the other. (*But SHE is succumbing to IDA's ministrations.*)

(*IDA arranges Katherine in her chair for the ritual brushing. IDA is good at this, she has been a professional hairdresser. SHE massages Katherine's hair with cologne, a towel spread over her shoulders, and KATHERINE visibly enjoys the process of being brushed and fussed over, and calms down.*)

IDA. (*Mutters soothing remarks such as.*) There ... Does that feel nice? Now we'll pat it this way ... Mmm ... Now some eau de cologne. Beautiful, beautiful hair, you've got, Katie. You look like a princess. Now like this ... Now we'll give it another rub ... Now we'll brush it through again ...

(*After a good deal of this, KATHERINE relaxes and takes a sip of the milk. Even when IDA buries her face in her hair, SHE is tolerant and gives her a gentle pat on the arm.*)

KATHERINE. When you've finished, you can tuck me in, if you like. Then I'll be sure that no mosquitoes get in with me.

IDA. (*Looking at Katherine in the mirror.*) Yes, of course I will. And now you look lovely, with your hair all soft. Is it comfortable? Or would you like something round it for the night?

KATHERINE. No, just like that, Ida dear. Thank you. You can take my kimono and hang it up, if you like.

(IDA does so, handling Katherine like precious goods, stroking down the skirt of her nightdress, carefully arranging the bed for her, etc., and KATHERINE submits to all this with considerable pleasure. As IDA pulls out the mosquito net, KATHERINE arranges it round herself like a bridal veil. SHE is camping it up.

KATHERINE. But I always wear black at weddings, Jones. And I'd like my drink of water before I'm shut in!

(IDA complies.)

KATHERINE. And don't forget to tuck in my feet.

(This too IDA does. Then SHE very carefully smooths the covers over Katherine, and closes the mosquito net around her. SHE stands looking.)

KATHERINE. Are you quite sure there aren't any inside the net?
IDA. I'll wait for a while, dear, just to be sure. You go to sleep if you can.
KATHERINE. If you don't mind, Jones. It's nice knowing you're there. You can turn off the light if you want to.

(SHE does so. IDA waits in the nearly dark room, outside the mosquito net. Inside it is the shrouded, immobile figure of Katherine. IDA sits at the table, and notices

the uneaten biscuits. After a while SHE picks one up,
then puts it down again.)

KATHERINE. (*Voice from inside the net.*) Go on,
Jonesie. No one is trying to poison *you*.

CURTAIN

ACT II

Scene 1

Dr. Bouchage's consulting room. KATHERINE is on the examination couch, sitting up as HE listens to her chest. SHE is wearing the cotton halter he provides for his examinations, and a skirt.

BOUCHAGE. Breathe deeply please ... Once more ... and now ... (*Etc.*) Now please would you cough, Mrs. Murry? And again ... Yes. Thank you. This gland in your neck is a little swollen, I notice. Yes ...

(When HE has finished and is making notes at his desk, KATHERINE lies back exhausted. HE approaches the examination couch again.)

BOUCHAGE. Now, Mrs. Murry, if you could lie quite flat, perhaps I might just feel your abdomen also ...
KATHERINE. Oh, doctor, isn't there *anything* I can keep to myself?
BOUCHAGE. (*Smiles kindly.*) You see, it is difficult to treat just one half of a patient. I will not hurt you at all. But it is important for me to understand your entire situation. If we are to make the cure together ...

43

(Reluctantly, but won over, KATHERINE slides down the couch. BOUCHAGE carefully covers her top half and her legs in order to examine her abdomen.)

BOUCHAGE. You have a scar here, I notice. Do you know what caused it?

KATHERINE. It's from an operation.

BOUCHAGE. When did you have this operation, Mrs. Murry?

KATHERINE. A long time ago. It was in 1909—or 1910. Yes, early in 1910.

BOUCHAGE. Do you have any idea what the operation was for?

KATHERINE. It was for peritonitis. It was very painful. I remember that. I had fever ... I couldn't lie straight, it hurt so much. Ida fetched me. She had to get a nurse.

BOUCHAGE. For peritonitis, you say? Have you any idea what the cause of the peritonitis was?

KATHERINE. Not really.

BOUCHAGE. *(Still pressing her abdomen.)* It was evidently not an appendix.

(KATHERINE looks at him silently.)

BOUCHAGE. *(Persists gently.)* Much pain, you say?

(KATHERINE nods mutely.)

BOUCHAGE. Forgive me, Mrs. Murry. Do you remember if you suffered from other symptoms about that time: a discharge, perhaps—perhaps a white discharge?

(KATHERINE nods again.)

BOUCHAGE. Do you remember if it continued for long?

KATHERINE. Months and months. I didn't know what was the matter. As you can imagine, it wasn't the sort of thing one discussed with anyone at all. Even now, frankly.

BOUCHAGE. Have you had recurrences of this type of trouble?

KATHERINE. Well, yes. From time to time.

BOUCHAGE. Excuse me, Mrs. Murry: do you find any connection between these recurrences and your ... intimate, personal life?

(Again, SHE nods.)

BOUCHAGE. And since then, no children, no pregnancies?

KATHERINE. *(Agonized, nods again.)* I sometimes thought I might be pregnant. I wanted children. I still want children, very much indeed!

BOUCHAGE. *(Still more gently, nodding.)* Mrs. Murry: this trouble began before your marriage?

KATHERINE. Perhaps I didn't tell you. I was married once before. When I was very young. That was when I had the baby who died, before this operation. I was in Bavaria. It was a very difficult time for me. *(SHE turns her head aside, deeply embarrassed.)* There were men there ... There was a man I trusted ... a Polish man ...

BOUCHAGE. (*HE is very interested, but also avoids looking at her face.*) *Ne vous affligez pas, madame*—do not be upset please, Mrs. Murry.

(*KATHERINE is now crying, but rigid and silent.*)

BOUCHAGE. These are not uncommon problems. It is better to know our enemy. Only then can we fight him, and make sure that he is not infiltrating in one place while we defend another. You will see that it is easier for us to progress against the tuberculosis if we understand the other aspects of your illness.

KATHERINE. (*Now behind the screen, dressing and struggling to compose herself.*) And can you help me to have a child? It's not too late, is it?

BOUCHAGE. (*Looking down at his notes.*) That is something we shall have to consider carefully. I don't think I can answer your question straight away.

(*HE makes some notes as KATHERINE continues to dress. When SHE emerges—and SHE is now using a stick—HE stands up and leads her gently to sit down opposite him again. HE speaks carefully, looking down at his notes at times.*)

BOUCHAGE. As you probably realize yourself, Mrs. Murry, some of your symptoms are not related to the weakness in your lungs. You were aware of them earlier, I believe—the rheumatic pains in your hip joints, in your hands and your feet, for example. You have had much pain from these. This pain began after the operation you were obliged to undergo when you were—let me see—when you were twenty-two. Probably you did not understand the reason for this operation. From what you have told me, and from what I observe, it seems likely that it was necessary to remove a part of your reproductive system because it was infected with a disease. You may not have heard of the disease. It is not usually mentioned to ladies, although it is a disease that can lead to the symptoms from which you have suffered. It is troublesome, and lowering; and it can make it difficult to bear children.

KATHERINE. (*Stony.*) Does this disease have a name?

BOUCHAGE. It is a venereal disease. Not the worst, by any means. It is called gonorrhea.

KATHERINE. Am I cured?

BOUCHAGE. You are cured in the sense that you have none of the primary symptoms. Unfortunately, you are left with the after-effects.

KATHERINE. You don't just mean the scar and the rheumatism?

BOUCHAGE. Not just the scar and the rheumatism, no.

KATHERINE. It's best to know. I suppose I half knew already. Something more to put down to experience. Oh, God. No one tells you. No one warns you. Not even Mother. It's not connected with my present illness, is it?

BOUCHAGE. No, no, not at all. The gods have attacked you twice, that is all.

KATHERINE. I'll allow the gods full responsibility for the tuberculosis ... Only the other disease—you could say it was my fault. (*Pause.*) So there's not too much left to hope for.

BOUCHAGE. That is never true.

KATHERINE. It is sometimes true, though doctors don't like to say so.

BOUCHAGE. It is certainly not true in your case, Mrs. Murry. I am sure that for you it is best to understand your own situation, and to proceed from your knowledge. (*Short pause, then HE speaks briskly.*) Meanwhile, I should like to treat the gland in your neck, to reduce the swelling. I could come to Isola Bella on Friday afternoon if that is convenient?

(KATHERINE, who has emerged, and is feeling her neck, nods mutely.)

BOUCHAGE. (*Smiles encouragingly.*) Miss Baker can offer me some five-o'clock English tea and show me her photograph album.

KATHERINE. I'm afraid there is nothing in it but pictures of me.

BOUCHAGE. That will make it all the more interesting. (*HE sees HER out.*)

ACT II

Scene 2

The terrace. The table is set for a festive lunch, with flowers, china and wine glasses. The meal is over, and there are opened presents: a bottle of scent, a silk petticoat, stockings, a small box of crystallized fruit, etc. KATHERINE and IDA are at the table;

KATHERINE is smoking a cigarette and drinking coffee. SHE is looking very disconsolate.

IDA. (*Investigating the crystallized fruit.*) Do you think this is a raspberry or a plum?

KATHERINE. Try it, Ida, and then you'll know.

IDA. You have one first, Katie. It's your birthday, you should start the box.

KATHERINE. I'm not sure I believe that being thirty-two years old is a cause for eating crystallized fruits. And I've already eaten too much lunch. But I'll have some more coffee.

IDA. Would you like to go for a drive in a *fiacre* this afternoon, if I can arrange it?

KATHERINE. (*Listlessly.*) I think I'll just sit here and think about things. You go, if you want to. I don't mind being alone.

(Pause while MARIE comes out to fetch some of the debris of the lunch and to observe her ladies.)

IDA. Perhaps I might try another of the fruits. They are very good.

KATHERINE. Why not? "The only way to get rid of temptation is to yield to it."

IDA. Just one then. (*SHE chooses one carefully.*) But what advice, Katie!

KATHERINE. I got it from Oscar Wilde. And have another, go on: "Push everything as far as it will go." Also Oscar Wilde.

IDA. No. I'm closing the box.

(Sound of DOORBELL. MARIE emerges, bustling happily, with a telegram on a tray.)

MARIE. *Pour madame! Un télégramme, madame!*
KATHERINE. *(Visibly pleased and excited, fishes in her purse for a coin.) Cinquante centimes pour le garçon!*

(SHE gives it to MARIE. IDA pulls a face at this wild extravagance, but is relieved that the telegram has arrived. KATHERINE, trying to appear unhurried, opens it. IDA watches. KATHERINE's face falls.)

KATHERINE. It's only some nonsense from my sister Chaddie.
IDA. Well, at least she's remembered.
KATHERINE. Who cares about sisters? That's the first time he's forgotten my birthday in eight years, Ida ...
IDA. I don't think men think about birthdays in the same way, you know.
KATHERINE. *(Taking no notice.)* And Ida: I've *still* not had that packet of letters. They must be lost. Or else he's thoroughly engrossed in reading them. *Ida!* I'm so completely helpless here! *(Pause.)* And another thing. He hasn't even sent me the money for my reviews. How does he think we manage here? *We* don't get asked out to dinner by Bloomsbury hostesses. We have to pay for our own dinners ... It's a bit cool of him just to pocket my earnings ... Why do men think they can do anything at all to us, and we'll never object or rebel?
IDA. *(Timidly at first, but gaining confidence as she goes on.)* Perhaps it would be best if you spent your working time on your own stories, and gave up the

reviewing. After all, you do get paid for stories; lots of magazines ask for them. Then you could have your own agent. It doesn't have to be Jack. You could deal directly with your agent, and your agent would pay you directly. It would make you freer.

KATHERINE. How absurd you are, Ida. You don't know anything about reviewing; or magazines; or agents.

IDA. (*Quietly pleased with herself.*) I do know Mr Lawrence has an agent. He told me so, when he came to see you in Hampstead.

KATHERINE. *Lawrence! Lawrence* told *you* about his *agent*? You had little chats with him on the stairs about literary matters?

IDA. (*Stubbornly.*) I liked him. And he seemed to like me. He sometimes came to talk to me downstairs. And he thought you should not depend so much on Jack.

KATHERINE. (*Flaring up.*) A fine one he is to preach to me—and a fine one you are, Jones, if it comes to that! I'll make my own decisions about my work, thank you. And I've never depended on Jack: not for a single penny. More often, he's been dependent on me, as you very well know. (*Pause. SHE lights another cigarette.*) All the same, he *must* send me those letters. I shan't forgive him if he doesn't fight Floryan to the death for me. (*Another pause. KATHERINE gets up and starts to pace the terrace, IDA hovering in her wake.*) I'll fight my illness. No one can fight on two fronts at the same time. (*With a flash of malice.*) Two—or three!

IDA. (*Very simply.*) The name of Mr. Lawrence's agent is James Pinker.

(KATHERINE stops, turns, looks at Ida. IDA, pleased with herself, goes into the house, leaving KATHERINE to consider this information.)

ACT II

Scene 3

Katherine's bedroom, daytime. SHE is in bed, pale and ill, in night things. We see DR. BOUCHAGE coming in, waiting downstairs, looking at Ida's photograph album. HE goes up to his patient. IDA is sitting on the terrace. HE smiles at KATHERINE, who gives him a stony look back.

KATHERINE. You have a bad patient today, doctor. Perhaps you are not such a good doctor as we both thought. I can hardly crawl across the room. But then I don't have much reason for wanting to crawl across the room, do I? Fever and headache, more headache, more fever. I can't work. My spine aches and aches. My feet and hands are unbearably painful. And now this gland in my neck. My proper life seems to be over. Am I *never* going to be any better than this?

BOUCHAGE. I am sorry you are going through such a bad and wearisome time, Mrs. Murry; of course I'll do everything that lies in my power to alleviate your symptoms. *(HE takes one or both of her hands and massages them while HE talks.)* But I believe you have strength in yourself to fight this disease. Maybe I am not such a good doctor as you hoped. I have to help you find a way to mobilize your strength. My impression at the moment is that you are fighting some other battles, and allowing the disease to take hold of you while your attention is distracted by these other, less important things.

KATHERINE. Of course I have other problems. I have my past life, like a perpetual reproach to the present. Of course I get very depressed. And I have no one to talk to. I am alone.

BOUCHAGE. What about Miss Baker? Can you not talk to her?

KATHERINE. (*Taking back her hands.*) Ida? Ida drives me mad. She can't *leave* me alone. She's like a ghoul, hanging over me, waiting for me to get worse so that ... She'd like me to be utterly dependent on her.

BOUCHAGE. (*Who is now standing up, turned away from Katherine.*) She is very attached to you. I think she would like you to be cured.

KATHERINE. Doctor Bouchage: your wedding ring is slipping on your finger today.

BOUCHAGE. It is always a little loose.

KATHERINE. It wasn't loose when you first examined me. Perhaps I should ask Ida to bring *you* a drink of milk.

(*BOUCHAGE doesn't like this.*)

KATHERINE. But I don't think you understand about Ida. She's always had this passion for me, since we were girls. She's jealous of my husband. She's even jealous of the cook. She's probably jealous of you. She wants to worship me, but there aren't to be any other worshippers at the shrine. If I were dead, she could have me all to herself. And then I shouldn't be horrible to her any more either.

BOUCHAGE. But this is your idea, Mrs. Murry, not Miss Baker's, about being dead. It is an idea you should put aside. There is no reason why you should not live many years still.

KATHERINE. I wonder whether you believe that yourself, Dr. Bouchage ... Well, I can see I must try not to quarrel with Miss Baker. But I am very lonely without my husband.

BOUCHAGE. He is still very busy in London? There is no chance that he might come and join you in Menton for a time?

KATHERINE. Of course he would *like* to come. But it is difficult for him. His work really requires his presence in England ... But we write to one another. We write every day. Well, *I* write every day. Sometimes I wonder if he reads all my letters. I hate the thought of people carrying round one's letters unopened in their pockets, don't you, because they are too busy to read them? Do you ever do that, Dr. Bouchage—I mean, keep somebody's letters unopened for a long time?

BOUCHAGE. I don't receive so many letters that I can treat them in this way. One wife, one child ...

KATHERINE. A happy man.

(BOUCHAGE makes an equivocal gesture.)

KATHERINE. But have you never had dozens and dozens of letters from someone, someone you are not interested in any more, and not known what to do with them?

BOUCHAGE. No, that has not happened to me. Perhaps it is only beautiful women who have this experience.

KATHERINE. Oh, it's happened to me. Quite often, even. I've done some dreadful things with letters. I've given letters from one man to another man to read. Would you do that?

BOUCHAGE. Some letters are private, some letters less private.

KATHERINE. Well, I've shown my husband letters from other men, in the past, before we were married. But then I've burnt them. Sometimes I wonder if he would do the same to me. He has lots of friends in London, you know, women he sees, who might like to read my letters, and laugh at my plight. Even when they are pretending to be my friends, some of them. Women like him, because he looks like a little boy, helpless. Only he's not helpless, really.

BOUCHAGE. Mrs. Murry, it would not be normal for a husband who loves his wife to show her letters to another person. It is not reasonable for you to imagine such things, to torment yourself with ideas of this kind.

KATHERINE. My husband and I don't have a normal relationship, Dr. Bouchage, you see. We have a very special sort of relationship. Oh, it's not that we don't love one another, we do. But we are not like other couples, not at all like the banker and his wife, or the lawyer and his wife—or even the doctor and his wife. We are writers, we live outside the rules.

BOUCHAGE. Yes. I see. Perhaps the rules are made for comfort, though? It is always more difficult and dangerous to live outside the rules. Even for writers. Maybe you need the comfort of rules now, so that you can give your energy to getting your health back. Perhaps you should invite your husband to come here to be with you for a time.

KATHERINE. I can't *ask* him for things. Never. Never. I never ask people for things. I do them for myself. He doesn't pay a penny for me, you know. If I didn't earn, I'd starve. I shouldn't be able to pay *your* bills, Dr. Bouchage.

BOUCHAGE. (*Somewhat taken aback by this.*) At least you are here, comfortably, with Miss Baker, who would not let you starve.

KATHERINE. (*Laughing.*) No, Ida would certainly not let me starve. Or herself. One meal after another, all day long, is Ida's regime.

BOUCHAGE. But that is excellent. It is exactly what you should be having. It proves how well Miss Baker understands your needs, and how well she furnishes them. Perhaps you have underestimated her capacities a little?

KATHERINE. Perhaps.

BOUCHAGE. She is helpful to you in your work? She saves you time and energy?

KATHERINE. The perfect companion, you mean? Almost as good as Madame Bouchage—with whom you never quarrel, I suppose.

BOUCHAGE. (*A flash of annoyance.*) I am not the patient, Mrs. Murry.

KATHERINE. (*Pleased to have stung him.*) Even the good doctor can be dissatisfied sometimes, I imagine. But yes, Ida does save my time and energy *sometimes*. Sometimes she exasperates me so much that I waste all my energy raging at her. The other day I was so furious with her that my face turned *green* with rage—actually, literally green. Greenish-black: I caught sight of it in the mirror, and felt quite frightened of myself.

BOUCHAGE. Today, however, you are not green, only rather pale. You want to strike and wound, but you should keep your energy for better things. What is it about kind Miss Baker that angers you so?

KATHERINE. You wouldn't understand, Doctor Bouchage. It's the whole history of our lives. An old story. A very long story.

BOUCHAGE. Let me guess something. Perhaps Miss Baker makes you angry because she is the wrong person in your mind; you would prefer it if your husband were here with you. If you can forgive Miss Baker the fact that she is not Mr. Murry, then you may not be so angry with her.

(KATHERINE hunches up and turns away from Bouchage, like a child.)

BOUCHAGE. If you are ready, Mrs. Murry, I should give you your injection, and also listen to your chest. I should be a poor doctor if I tired you out with talking.

(HE opens his bag and begins to prepare his things. KATHERINE turns back toward him and prepares herself for the medical procedures, with the air of someone bracing themselves for torture. As HE is injecting her and then saying his farewell, we see that downstairs IDA is hovering, rearranging the flowers and papers in the salon, and MARIE has come in and is simply standing looking up the stairs where she knows the doctor is with Katherine.)

MARIE. *Cette pauvre petite Madame, elle souffre vraiment beaucoup. Esperons que le docteur lui fasse un peu de bien aujourd' hui, n' est-ce pas, Meess Jones?*

IDA. Marie: my name is Baker, Mademoiselle Baker, as I have told you already.

MARIE. (*Not without malice.*) *Oh, je m'excuse, Mademoiselle Baker, c'est à cause de Madame, vous comprenez, qui vous appelle toujours "Jones". Alors en Angleterre, vous vous appelez "Mees Baker"?*

IDA. (*Irritably, distracted.*) Yes, yes.

MARIE. *Il faut dire que c'est Monsieur Jack, son mari, dont elle a besoin—"the 'usband"—plutôt que le docteur, vous ne trouvez pas, Mees?*

IDA. Madame needs *repos* and *nourriture*. Those are what she needs, as Dr. Bouchage has said. And the *nourriture* is your province, Marie. Thank you. (*SHE indicates that she expects Marie to depart kitchenwards.*)

MARIE. (*Leaving reluctantly.*) *Ah, ma pauvre petite Madame. Je fais de mon mieux, mais c'est bien triste de la voir toujours maigrir.*

(*IDA continues to move about without any real purpose until BOUCHAGE comes slowly down the stairs. HE shakes her hand.*)

BOUCHAGE. Miss Baker. Your friend is very tired this afternoon, and low spirited. But she will improve in a few days.

IDA. I find it hard to see her suffer.

BOUCHAGE. It is *the* most difficult thing. But you are able to help her.

IDA. I should like to. More often I exasperate her.

BOUCHAGE. Yes. Sometimes whoever is with her is not the right person. That is the nature of the illness. Whoever is there will exasperate her. Of course, someone else would be better. A different doctor, a different friend, a different kind of affection. You must try not to feel it, not to notice even. That is one way of helping—of relieving her. Believe me, you are not the wrong person. Stay with her. She is going to need you still more ... And for now, let her sleep, and eat whatever she likes. Cigarettes and coffee are not so good, but if she wants them ...

IDA. Doctor Bouchage. When you say she is going to need me still more, are you telling me that she is not going to get better?

BOUCHAGE. No doctor would tell you such a thing, Miss Baker. I simply mean that you are a necessary friend and companion; and perhaps not just for the winter months. A chronic illness requires a constant friend—and that I know you are. Steadfast, constant Miss Baker. (HE takes her hand and shakes it.) I shall see you and Mrs. Murry in two days, or sooner if you need me. (And HE goes.)

(IDA stands still, thinking. MARIE peeps out of the kitchen.)

IDA. (Suddenly registers her presence. Inspired into French.) Marie—Il faut travailler ... all of us together ... we must get her well again ... guérir Madame. Tous, tous. Doctor Bouchage. Et vous. Et moi. Il faut.

(MARIE hardly knows what to make of this, but shrugs and smiles, and allows IDA to enter the kitchen with HER.)

ACT II

Scene 4

The terrace, beyond the chaise longue, which has in any case been put away because autumn has set in and there has been a cold spell. It is evening. KATHERINE, bundled up warmly over her night things, is standing over a small BONFIRE, watching the last of a bundle of letters fall into ash. IDA comes from the house to join her.

KATHERINE. That's done, at last. And I hope every letter I've ever written will meet the same fate. Remember that, Jones. It's an order.

IDA. You know I'd never reveal anything about you to anyone, Katie. I wouldn't and couldn't do such a thing. Private is private.

KATHERINE. And if you do, I'll come and haunt you. I'll send you a coffin worm in a matchbox from beyond the grave, just to show you.

(IDA is not sure how to take this, but attempts a brave smile.)

KATHERINE. But of course Jack is saving up all my letters—he actually *asked* me to keep his for posterity, in case we turn out to be the Keats and Shelley of our generation. Or perhaps he's Wordsworth and I'm Dorothy. Poor Jack.

IDA. Not poor Jack at all. I only hope he is worthy of you, and of your trust in him.

KATHERINE. It certainly took him a long time to make up his mind to part with Floryan's letters. I suppose he read them. And do you know, he hasn't even sent me a copy of my own book yet? I expect he's kept the six free copies for his collection, in case they become valuable items. Well, I'm not doing any more reviewing for him, I can tell you.

IDA. Quite right, Katie, I'm very glad to hear you say that at last. Dr. Bouchage has been telling you to stop for weeks.

KATHERINE. And I'm not going to keep a journal any more either. You're supposed to tell the truth in a journal, and I simply daren't try to tell the truth any more. From now on, I intend to write only stories. There's going to be one called *Poison*. It will be about a very loving couple.

IDA. (*Not taking this in.*) That's good, Katie. And you must have rest, and good food—and true friends, I hope.

KATHERINE. Oh, I'm tired. Suddenly. I can hardly stand up, Jones. I think you're going to have to help me in.

IDA. Of course, of course. Here I am. It's your bedtime in any case.

KATHERINE. (*Laughing, but weakly.*) Is it a hot drink, or a cold drink tonight?

IDA. Well: it's *meant* to be hot, but it soon may be cold, if we don't get you to bed quickly.

(KATHERINE takes Ida's arm and THEY go slowly towards the house together. KATHERINE turns to look back at the remains of her bonfire.)

KATHERINE. So much for *that* bit of the past. At least that won't rise up and haunt me now.

(And THEY go up together to Katherine's bedroom. SHE climbs into bed, IDA prepares to tuck her up, but KATHERINE remains sitting up and holds onto her, and as SHE tries to shut off the light says:)

KATHERINE. No, Ida, don't. I have been having such peculiar dreams, Jones. Jones. I must tell you. They were so vivid, I thought they were really happening, here. Almost like a message. I was alone, but there was a huge crowd, in Piccadilly Circus I think. It was a black night. There were drunks, and one said to me, "You're corrupt. You've played the lady once too often ..." And I saw the sky was changed. A man shouted out, "There are six moons." And I saw that there *were* six moons. It was the end of the world. Someone came in a horse and cart. It was the Salvation Army, with a woman doling out tracts. (*A whisper only.*) And she gave me one, and asked me, "Are you corrupted, Katherine?" And there was ash falling, thick ash, falling all over the crowd, all over all of us. Yes. Ashes.

IDA. (*Somewhat shaken by this.*) It was just a bad dream, Katie.

KATHERINE. Ida. Sometimes I miss Jack so badly. I miss him. I *long* for him.

IDA. I know, I understand ...

KATHERINE. And sometimes ... I don't care a *rap!*

ACT II

Scene 5

Upstairs, IDA is helping KATHERINE to dress while MARIE brings in a tray of coffee for Bouchage downstairs. As KATHERINE starts down the stairs, IDA adds a brightly colored silk scarf to conceal the gland in her neck. KATHERINE goes down, MARIE and IDA go off.

KATHERINE. (*As DR. BOUCHAGE shakes her hand.*) No miracles from me, I'm afraid, Doctor Bouchage. I'm still coughing. In fact I'm coughing more than ever. I keep Ida awake half the night, through the wall. My weight has gone down another two pounds this week. And your injections make it a matter of some difficulty to sit down for more than a few minutes at a time ... Oh, dear. Then the gland in my neck has become very tender—I can feel the blood throbbing in it all the time ... especially at night.

BOUCHAGE. We must try to relieve that, Mrs. Murry. Do not be too despondent. If you find the injections more uncomfortable than you can bear, we need not continue with them. There are other possibilities of treatment. And I can give you something different for your cough.

KATHERINE. And my two pounds? Can you give me back my two pounds of flesh?

BOUCHAGE. If you will rest more, and eat more, there is no reason why you should not put on weight again. No reason at all. I hope you are not persisting in working too hard, Mrs. Murry. It is not advisable in your present state of health; not at all advisable.

KATHERINE. But I must live, Doctor.

BOUCHAGE. (*Shrugs slightly.*) Mrs. Murry, you are full of life—believe me, you are more alive than most of my patients—only you must cherish your own life more than you do. You must preserve yourself. (*Pause.*) I have been meaning to say to you that I would not advise you to stay in Menton much longer.

KATHERINE. Not stay in Menton? I thought it was meant to be the best place for me?

BOUCHAGE. In winter, perhaps ... although even then ... But when the weather gets warmer again, emphatically not. I should advise you to go north, into the mountains, in the spring. There are excellent doctors there, and I can give you a letter to take with you. In summer, there is nothing good about this coast for you, believe me. Mrs. Murry: please take my advice in this matter. Please ask your good companion—Miss Baker—to take you to Savoie or Switzerland, and stay there. Stay in one place, and do not work. Even if you will not go to a sanatorium, at least rest. Perhaps your husband will be able to join you for the summer. But if I were you I should keep Miss Baker with you, to give you the care you require. I should like to think of you living comfortably, and I believe she knows how to look after you quite well.

KATHERINE. Miss Baker. (*Laughing.*) You want me to lose a husband and gain a wife. I shall have to think about all this. (*Pause.*) Dr. Bouchage, I told you that I am a writer. I have, on your advice, given up the work I was doing for my husband's magazine. That doesn't matter. But now I have to write *for myself*. You understand what I mean? You have seen me over these months at Menton. You know something about me—something of my temperament, something of my history; some of the bad things that have happened to me. I have things I want to write. *If* I do not have long to live, I want to spend the time I have in saying—or in starting to say—what I know about the world. About men and women. About human indifference and cruelty and stupidity. About the way in which people devour one another, and poison one another. About the importance of hate. (*Pause.*) There are so many things I want to describe! What it is to like to be an ordinary, healthy woman—Marie, say, going to the market under the green and gold shade of the plane trees, through streets that smell of lemons and fresh coffee—past cafes where lovers who imagine they are happy are sitting under the pink and white umbrellas—past the fountain where she stops to talk to other ordinary, healthy women with their water pots—feeling on their faces and arms the warm wind off the sea. The treacherous sea. All this, all this: and to know in your own bones nothing but suffering and death.

(*Pause. BOUCHAGE is looking at her intently, and listening.*)

KATHERINE. And you, Doctor Bouchage: you know very well what I mean, I believe. All this time you have been plumbing my depths, finding out my secrets, I have been observing you too, and finding out yours. You may be the doctor, but I am the writer. And just as you can tell me things about myself, I can tell you something about yourself. You know that my life is burning away—more or less quickly—but I know that you are also touched by the same burning frost.

(BOUCHAGE, who has been listening intently, is extremely disconcerted, and holds up his hand, but SHE continues.)

KATHERINE. I can see it in your eyes and feel it when you touch me with your good, sensitive fingers. You are too quick, too kind, too responsive, too eager. If you are a good doctor, it is because you are almost as sick as I am.

BOUCHAGE. You are an observant woman, Mrs. Murry, as well as a gifted one.

KATHERINE. And are *you* going north, Doctor Bouchage? Which mountains are you going to settle in? Or are you going to stay here with Madame Bouchage and your little son, in the treacherous bright sunshine, beside the treacherous bright sea, for as long as the burning frost allows you? Enjoying your life and your work, in the company of the people you love best, for as long as the gods permit?

(BOUCHAGE is now looking down and will not raise his eyes to meet those of Katherine.)

KATHERINE. I recognize you, and you recognize me, because we are the same, Doctor Bouchage. We have both been corrupted by something bad. Consumption—tuberculosis—whatever name it bears. And neither of us is likely to escape from the bad things that have entered into us. But I'll do as you say. I'll go to Switzerland with Miss Baker, and I'll let her look after me. I'll take your letter humbly and gratefully, in which you pass on to another doctor all the things you have found out about my illnesses—my disgraceful scars and symptoms, all the sins of my youth laid bare. One thing I shall not promise you, though.

(Now BOUCHAGE looks up.)

KATHERINE. I do not intend to give up my work. On the contrary, I intend from now on to work harder than I have ever worked in my life.

BOUCHAGE. I salute you, Mrs. Murry, and your courage. As long as you are in Menton I shall be happy to be of service to you. But I believe you yourself will now make your own salvation.

KATHERINE. *(Laughing.)* We shall see. We shall tell one another in heaven. If I get there first, I shall look out for you and tell the angels to prepare a good place for the good doctor.

(SHE laughs, and coughs, and laughs, and after a moment of hesitation, BOUCHAGE joins in the laughter.)

ACT II

Scene 6

Night. Katherine's bedroom. Downstairs, IDA has fallen asleep in her chair. We hear a CLOCK strike four. KATHERINE is sitting in her bed writing furiously and almost hypnotically, in a trance of concentration, dashing off the sheets with scarcely a pause or correction. After a while SHE finishes, holds the last sheet away from her, puts it down on the pile of finished pages. SHE is exhausted and elated, her face full of triumph. Then SHE calls out.

KATHERINE. Jones! Jones! Come at once, please, Jones!

(IDA wakes, shakes herself, rushes upstairs, sleep in her eyes, confused and worried.)

IDA. Here I am—Kass—what is it?
KATHERINE. It's finished! It's finished, Jonesie, we must celebrate. Really, it's the best thing I've ever done, I think. There you are. It might almost be about you—well, not you, of course, but you as you might have been if you had never met me—if you'd just gone on being constant to your father instead of me—Ida Constance—the well-named. *(KATHERINE is high on her achievement.)*
IDA. *(Gently.)* You *have* worked hard, Katie. Nearly through the night. You must be worn out ... completely worn out. Well done, though. I'm never clever enough to understand your stories properly, but I certainly want to

read this one. "The Daughters of the Late Colonel." (*SHE sits on the bed, knocking the pile of papers to the floor as she does so.*) Oh, dear, now what have I done? How could I be so utterly stupid and clumsy? I *am* so sorry, truly sorry, Kass dear.

KATHERINE. (*For once does not seem to be exasperated.*) Oh, they're quite safe, just put them back on the bed and I'll sort them out while you make the tea. Tea and *lemon*, don't you think, at this hour of the morning, and—Ida what about some egg sandwiches while we're about it? Real English food! I'm so *hungry*.

IDA. Yes, of course, we'll have a feast. A celebration.

KATHERINE. Wonderful! Oh, Ida, what would I do without you—you're the real friend—you're the perfect friend—more than a friend. You know what you are, you're what every woman needs: you're my true wife.

(*IDA's face is transformed with emotion she cannot express.*)

KATHERINE. Yes, well, before you get too serious, let's say I'm William and you're Dorothy. Right, wife, now, off to make the tea and sandwiches. Perfect, mind, don't forget the salt, or else ...

(*IDA hurries off downstairs to the kitchen. While she is there, KATHERINE sorts her scattered pages. As she does so, SHE reads aloud assorted passages from the story. SHE is high, very pleased with it all. It is growing LIGHTER.*)

KATHERINE. (*Reading from her own manuscript, savoring every word, acting it out.*)

> Josephine had had a moment of absolute terror at the cemetery, while the coffin was lowered, to think that she and Constantia had done this thing without asking his permission. What would father say when he found out? For he was bound to find out sooner or later. He always did. "Buried. You two girls had me *buried*!" She heard his stick thumping ... She heard him absolutely roaring, "And do you expect me to pay for this gimcrack excursion of yours?" "Oh," groaned poor Josephine aloud, "we shouldn't have done it, Con!" ... "Done what, Jug?" "Let them bu-bury father like that."... "But what else could we have done?... We couldn't have kept him, Jug... At any rate, not in a flat that size." (*More turning of pages.*) Yes, this is a good bit: "The sunlight pressed through the windows, thieved its way in, flashed its light over the furniture and the photographs ... When it came to mother's photograph ... it lingered as though puzzled to find so little remained of mother, except the earrings shaped like tiny pagodas and a black feather boa. As soon as a person was dead their photograph died too. ..."

Yes. Yes!

(*During this last passage, IDA is returning with a loaded tray, teapot, cups, napkins, plate of sandwiches, pieces of lemon. SHE hears it and smiles appreciatively and a shade ruefully. SHE struggles to find a place on the rumpled bed, then turns off the LIGHT in the room,*

*because the SUN has risen. KATHERINE stacks her
story and puts it carefully into a drawer. IDA pours the
tea. BOTH WOMEN eat and drink enthusiastically,
talking with their mouths full.)*

KATHERINE. What lovely, lovely sandwiches, Ida
Constance.

IDA. Marie had left some eggs already cooked.

KATHERINE. Delicious! And pepper, too. And lemon
tea. Just exactly what I need.

IDA. And I managed the spirit stove for the kettle.

KATHERINE. Bliss. This reminds me of school.
Feasts in bed. No grown man ever appreciates how good
food tastes in bed. But can we ever have been fifteen, Ida?
Just think, girls of fifteen, how perfect they can be—just
budding, so eager, so *avid* for everything. So pleased with
themselves. With such appetites. With this great expanse
of time in front of them.

IDA. You had a nightdress with tiny yellow flowers all
over it. And a blue silk dressing gown from Marshall &
Snelgrove.

KATHERINE. But it's better than those old times at
college now, though, don't you think? I mean, we are
really ourselves now, aren't we? Listen, Ida. We *must* be
happy together now. No more blackness from me. No
more—*silliness* from you. You can be very, very silly. But
there are to be no more makeshifts, no failures from now
on. I'm writing—I'm writing well. No reason why we
shouldn't be happy. Perhaps I shall spare six months a year
for Jack (*Her eye lights on the photograph.*)—to keep him
happy—because I do love him in spite of all—and six with
you—and we'll share everything. Let's see: we'll have tea

in forest glades, and go swimming in—Corsica, why not Corsica, don't you long to go there? In the afternoons, we'll attend concerts in public gardens. We'll have picnics on rocks by the sea—anything we have a fancy to do—and I'll work and work, and earn money for us. And I'll be famous—scandalously famous. You'll see.

IDA. Do you remember—in Chelsea—you said that I could be a tall green pillar, like a tree, and that you would be a bird—because you had so much to see and do—and that you'd always fly away from me, but when you were tired, you would come back and rest on the tree.

KATHERINE. (*Who perhaps doesn't remember really.*) Yes, yes, perhaps I did. But now ... how about two boats, sailing down the same river: that's more like it, don't you think? Two boats, sailing and sailing down the river ... (*SHE begins to talk to herself.*) Only we don't know how far it is to the sea ... Ida: you must clear all this up, we must get the crumbs out of the bed, and I must get some rest. What an idea! Egg sandwiches! You're quite crazy, you know, Jones. I'm absolutely *exhausted* all of a sudden. Only a few hours till lunch! How shall we do justice to Marie's *déjeuner*? You'll have to eat for two. (*More peals of laughter.*)

ACT II

Scene 7

A railway platform, somewhere between Menton and Switzerland. DIM LIGHT. KATHERINE and IDA are

sitting together on their luggage. KATHERINE, more
gaunt than ever, is packed round with cushions.

KATHERINE. I think I must be the best travelled
woman in Europe. There is nothing I don't know about
platforms, trains, stations, *couchettes*, timetables, buffets,
waiting rooms ... Waiting rooms! Well, off to a new life.
New rooms, new doctors, new cooks ... (*Then
affectionately, patting her.*) Same old Ida. Same old Jones.

IDA. I don't suppose I'll change much ... for the worse,
or for the better.

KATHERINE. The trouble with you, Jonesie, is you
are so damnably self-sacrificing. You never ask for a pound
of flesh back—and when I think of the pounds of flesh I
keep losing!

IDA. You'll put on weight again in Switzerland. There
are better doctors there. Bouchage wasn't really much use,
was he?

KATHERINE. What I like about you is that you
understand, but you don't understand too much. Bouchage
was a good doctor. Perhaps he grew rather unprofessionally
fond of me, but I'll forgive him that. Patients have to
flatter doctors, and doctors have to flatter patients. The
same as cooks. And he laughed at my jokes. Even my
limericks (*And SHE chants, in a silly voice, guying the
New Zealand accent.*)

The patient, who hailed from New Zealing,

Said: "Pray don't consider my feeling.

Provided you're certain

Twill not go on hurtin',

I'll lie here and smile at the ceiling.

(SHE laughs. IDA laughs.)

IDA. Katie!

(KATHERINE's laughter turns into a coughing bout. Her eyes are frightened as SHE struggles with it. IDA fumbles in one of the bags for a water bottle.)

IDA. There. There. When you're ready for some water.

(KATHERINE gestures her away. IDA searches again, finds a sponge, moistens it with the water, prepares to hold it to Katherine's brow and neck when she wants it. The fit subsides, IDA ministers to her, first with the sponge, then with the water.)

KATHERINE. *(Very slowly.)* Ohhhh. Oh, God. Oh, God. I thought for a minute ...
    IDA. All right, Katie love. All right. All right.
    KATHERINE. *(As SHE begins to recover her breath.)* I want to have time to do something more. Something better. You won't leave me, will you, Ida? I can't really write unless you're there to hold the fort.
    IDA. You know I shan't leave you as long as you want me. *(Brightly.)* And if you send me away in the summer, I'll keep a bag packed up to come at a moment's notice. You'll only have to send a telegram, and I'll be on my way.
    KATHERINE. Yes. I think you would put a girdle round the earth for me, wouldn't you? *(Then, in her dreamy voice.)* I know you'll do everything you can to help me. I know you're coming with me today. But quite soon,

there'll be a day like this, with sunshine and ordinary noises outside, trees coming into blossom, young people shouting across the street to each other, playing tennis ... trains arriving at platforms and leaving in exactly the same way as today ... only I'll be dying, and then dead. Nothing else will stop, only me, just like that. And then, Jonesie, you'll be the widow. (*Teasing her, beginning to enjoy her vision now.*) You'll be able to tell all, and become famous.

(*IDA shakes her head sadly.*)

KATHERINE. No, perhaps you *will* write about me ... reveal all my black secrets. I'll be nothing, and you can be someone for ever after. Perhaps you'll live to be ninety. Think of it, Ida! (*Wondering at the thought herself.*) Just think of it, Ida! (*KATHERINE leans away, half sleeping, and the LIGHT lowers on her, leaving IDA illuminated.*)

IDA. And I did live to be ninety. Years and years of widowed summer. Katherine died in ... let me see, in 1923. It wasn't spring. There was no blossom, no one playing tennis. It was January, a very cold winter. She ran up a flight of stairs, and died like a bird at the top.

After she died, Jack—her husband—grew rich on her stories, and on publishing her private journals and letters— all the ones she asked him to destroy.

(*Doing her best to be fair.*) He gave his version. And he married again—I should say, he married over and over again, because he had at least four wives ... Some of them were quite decent women.

I never married. For me, no one ever equalled Katie. There was something golden about her. Her voice. Her eyes. Her way of being. She could be cruel, but that came from her suffering. I kept her memory. And, after fifty years, I did write about her, just as she said I might. Although I thought I'd burnt them all, as she asked me, I found I had a few letters after all. When she died, there was an unposted letter to me on her table. It ended, "Write and tell me how you are, will you? Dear Ida?'"

Now the world knows all about her. And Katie's family, which had been so ashamed of her, and thought her wicked, discovered she was a genius, and grew proud of her after all. And people read her stories. All over the world.

But she was my Katie. And I was her Jones. (*Considering*.) She expressed herself in writing, and I expressed myself in service. I was her wife, and then her widow. Golden Katie, and Jones with the grey legs ...

(*And we hear the voice of:*)

KATHERINE. Jones! Jones! Get on with it, do.

CURTAIN

www.ingramcontent.com/pod-product-compliance
Lightning Source LLC
Chambersburg PA
CBHW070356120726
47909CB00008B/2874